THE RAINY-DAY CAT

Written and illustrated
by Kathy Wilburn

A GOLDEN BOOK · NEW YORK
Western Publishing Company, Inc., Racine, Wisconsin 53404

Fanny stared out the window at the gloomy day and wrinkled her whiskers. She yawned and stretched, then with a twitch of her tail looked for something to do.

A rackety sound drifted down from the attic. On soft padded paws Fanny climbed the stairs. Up and up she crept, the noise growing louder.

There was Shannon, building a kite! Fanny sat down in the middle of a big piece of crinkly paper that had a butterfly painted on it. "No, Fanny," said Shannon, picking her up and hugging her.

Shannon taped the butterfly picture onto two sticks crossed like a letter *t.* As Fanny looked on, she imagined sailing…

on a tall wooden ship…through time and space.

Perched high on a windowsill, Fanny watched the sky grow dark. A streak of silver split the air. To Fanny, the roaring thunder sounded like a dragon's bellow.

Poor Godfrey yelped and raced under the bed. "That dog is such a ninny," Fanny thought.

"Why, I'd like to climb right up to that dragon's lair and tame the old rascal with my magic violin!"

The wind smacked the roof, and in a flash
Fanny found Alex.

She crept close and curled up beside him.
While stroking her silky fur, Alex read her a tale of
a wise spell-casting wizard.

"Those magical spells are a breeze," she purred, "when done with a wand and a wondrous word...."

Rain fell in a loud clatter and pelted the windows. Snug within, Fanny peered at the goldfish swimming around and around in their glass bowl.

Watching them dart through castles and hide behind rocks, she drifted into a dream.

She floated beneath the sea, where merry
dolphins had parties and served green cake
with tea....

Fanny wondered if the rain would ever end.
She poked her nose through the torn screen in the
kitchen door. Water splashed onto the porch,
making little streams and pools. A leaf swirled past
with a small spider clinging to it.

"How exciting it would be," thought Fanny,
"to be rafting on a churning river...."

The rain had slowed to a soft, misty shower.
Fanny discovered a half-open door and peeked
inside. It was quiet and dark and a little bit scary.

But Fanny loved an adventure. So she bravely
set forth to explore the terrain....

The storm was over. Gardens glistened and smelled of fresh earth.

Godfrey bounded for the door, with
Shannon and Alex close behind.

"Here, kitty, come along to the backyard with us," they called to Fanny.

But Fanny only licked her paws and smoothed her whiskers.

"No, thank you," she thought, curling up in a sunny window. "It has been quite a long day."